Anna in Tuscany

a novella

STEPHANIE
VERNI

Anna in Tuscany is a work of fiction. All people and places are used fictitiously. Resemblances to actual persons, living or dead, events, locales, or establishments are coincidental.

All rights reserved. No part of this book may be reproduced in any form or by any means without the prior written consent of Mimosa Publishing, excepting brief quotes for reviews.

Book cover designed by Stephanie Verni.

ISBN 9798878798402

Copyright © 2021, 2024   by Stephanie Verni
All rights reserved.

For lovers of Italy, wine, food, spending time with family and friends, but mostly, for those who love love...

and a good cannoli.

Books by Stephanie Verni

Beneath the Mimosa Tree
Baseball Girl
Inn Significant
Little Milestones
The Postcard
Anna in Tuscany - A Novelette
From Humbug to Humble
The Letters in the Books - Coming Soon

Visit stephanieverni.com for more information

Anna in Tuscany

a novel

STEPHANIE
VERNI

– Chapter 1 –

I remembered a story my late grandmother, Nana, told me years ago about how lucky the number seven was for her. She married my grandfather, Vittore, (seven letters in his name) during a light snowfall on the seventh of January (a month with seven letters) in Livorno, Tuscany, (a town and region each containing seven letters), where they raised seven children and lived for many years before moving to the United States. It was one of those stories she would tell frequently, laughing about how ironic it was that her life had seemed to be determined by all things related to the number seven.

Incidentally, Nana's name was Arianna (seven letters), and I was named after her, although I am called Anna, a shortened version of the name we share.

Like a movie playing in my head, I pictured her sitting around our large dining table, her animated face telling that story the night I sat on a small suitcase begging it to close, the contents of it stuffed with clothing and reminders of my life here in America. In a matter of hours, I would board a flight at 7 p.m. on Friday, January 7, with the intention to live in Italy for a full year.

I wondered if Nana would think this meant my luck would change.

"Anna," my father shouted up the stairs. "We've got to get going or you'll be late, and check-in takes forever at this hour!"

"I'm coming," I said.

As I looked around my apartment for the last time, most of my belongings already moved into a storage facility down the road—my father and my brother promising to move the remainder of my things out after I'd gone—I swallowed hard. And while it was a big leap for me to leave my immediate family for twelve months, Italy was a second home to my parents. They were the ones who had pushed me to study abroad in Rome during college.

Life throws us unexpected curve balls, and at the age of thirty-three, my editor approached me about the opportunity to plant myself in Italy and write about its various regions. I'd been writing travel pieces for the magazine and website for three years, when the idea came to my editor to have me live in Italy. When I mentioned having family there—and possibly a place to hang my hat for while—I'd been selected as the obvious choice to go. Plus, it didn't hurt that I spoke a little Italian.

The family apartment in Siena had just been emptied, as the previous renters moved out at the end of December, and my mother's sister Rosa was more than happy for me to take on the lease. Rosa, who lived in our family's long-standing home in Tuscany, and who was busy with her own children and grandchildren, in addition to caring for my great aunt—my grandmother's sister—was pleased to know that a family member would be the renter. It lessened her burden to find a tenant.

"It will be such fun, let me tell you!" my mother had said to me when I had shared the news of the magazine's offering. "Not only will it give you time to clear your head and to write, but you'll also get to spend some time with your extended family who lives in Siena."

Once the logistics had been settled, I was now Rosa's favorite American relative. The added bonus for Rosa was that my mother—her sister—planned to come for a visit during the year. The idea of a large family reunion in the summer made everyone happy.

However, that was not the only reason I jumped

at the chance to set myself up in Italy; it also had to do with the fact that my dating life was an absolute disaster and finding the right match for me had become nearly impossible. I longed to have children and a family of my own, but luck had not been on my side. As I attended wedding after wedding of my friends over the last several years, I had yet to find someone who suited me—intellectually, passionately, and spiritually. I also traveled way too much for my job, and it was difficult to meet someone who could tolerate my work schedule. I was looking forward to having Tuscany as my home base in Italy, and I would venture out from there for day trips or an overnight stay, my editor's list of possible story ideas to cover for the magazine saved on my laptop.

"Got everything?" my father asked me as we closed the door behind us, knowing we had to get moving to get to the airport on time.

"I think so."

"It will be an adventure, Anna. Enjoy it," he said, patting me on the back.

I'd never taken less time to make a big life decision, and I prayed my time in Italy would be a good choice.

And for seven seconds, as Dad tossed the luggage into his car, I second-guessed the decision to go.

— Chapter 2 —

By the time the plane touched down in Italy, I felt exhausted and disheveled. Sleeping on a plane was never in the cards for me when flying, no matter how hard I tried. You would think I'd be used to flying by now.
The magazine had treated me to a car and driver to take me from the airport in Rome to Siena.
By some miracle, I found the driver. Luckily, he spoke a little English, so we were able to communicate better than I expected. His name was Jaco, a middle-aged man, tall and thin, with very tanned skin, and thick salt and pepper hair that he combed like Cary Grant. His voice sounded as if he'd smoked too many cigarettes over the years. I learned that he and his family live outside Rome. After exchanging a few pleasantries and pulling my sunglasses out of my carry-on bag and placing them on my face, the light of the morning sun blinding me, we began the drive north toward Tuscany.

Despite my eyelids feeling heavy, I couldn't close them for fear of missing out on the gorgeous scenery outside the car windows. The reality sunk in—*I was in Italy*. As we climbed the hills of Tuscany, my heart leapt with excitement at the prospect of returning to Rome and Venice and other regions for my assignments. I was lucky I only had my purse and one carry-on suitcase to contend with presently; my mother and I had shipped all my necessary things to Italy weeks prior in care of Rosa.

Jaco wound up the curved roads, as rolling hills and villas on large parcels of land came into view. There was no mistaking the architecture of the Tuscan homes in muted terracotta colors that matched the earth's natural tones. It was a beautiful winter day. Patches of small vineyards, farmland, and olive trees graced the land, and hilltop towns sat majestically on the peaks of rolling greenery. I asked Jaco if I could roll down the window for a moment and inhale the fresh air. He laughed.

"Do you not hav-a dis type o' fresh air where you live, Miss Anna?" he asked.

"No, we do, but not this type of landscape. It's gorgeous," I said, practically hanging my head out of the window like a dog. I snapped a quick photo as he drove.

"And-a-you stay a-while?" he asked.

"Yes, I'll be writing about Italy. I consider myself very lucky, Jaco."

"Ah, and-a taste-a de wine. D'good-a life, right Miss Anna?"

"Right," I said. I longed to taste the wine, eat the bread, and walk the streets of Siena.

The temperature reminded me of the weather we were having on the East Coast, hovering around fifty-three degrees. Despite it being winter, the sun warmed my face after being trapped on an airplane for so long. I had never grown accustomed to flying. I tried my hardest not to think about what the captain was up to in the cockpit, and I listened to the engines the entire time, making sure they sounded solid for the long flight. It was always the same with me—when the plane landed safely, I could go about my life without that worry.

I looked at my cell phone and saw a text from my mother.

It's Mom. Make it okay? As if I didn't know it was her.

I typed back, *Yes. It's marvelous.*

Good. Text me when you get into the apartment. xx, Mom

My mother never realized that you didn't have to sign off on a text, and I never told her. I found it charming that she always ended her texts like that.

*

When Jaco pulled up to the walled city, I was confident I knew which streets would take me to my new residence. My map reading skills were on point as I had grown into a seasoned travel writer over the last few years. I marked the streets that would take me to the apartment. Hence, this was why my carry-on suitcase had some wheels. It was going to be a little bit of a walk. Rosa had said she received my shipment of clothing and items, so I would have to go to her villa to pick them up. I had a of clothes in my suitcase that included my toothbrush, toothpaste, soap and shampoo, and contact lenses to make it through the day until I could fetch my clothing and various other essentials I had shipped to Italy from America. It was amazing how few material possessions one really needed to get by.

After I settled with Jaco and he profusely wished

me well, I entered the city of Siena. The walled city had a medieval feel. At one time, Florence and Siena were true rivals, and I expect for some, they still are, but Siena has such a different feel from Florence, and I distinctly remembered this from my days visiting when I was a teenager.

Rosa's apartment was just off of the Piazza Il Campo, the famous square that hosts the annual Palio horse race, with the tall tower that majestically dons the square. I stopped for a second and checked myself. I was actually here. Standing on Siena's rich grounds, the streets were alive with people walking, laughing, talking, or drinking coffee, even on a January day. I passed restaurants where people were sitting at windows enjoying a glass of wine, and pasticerrias and coffee shops appeared warm and inviting. I was immediately engulfed by the smells of food wafting out onto the streets and mingling with the scent of cappuccino as I marveled at the romance of the city.

Italy…I have missed you.

I continued to follow the walking map on my GPS, and it guided me perfectly to Via delle Campagne. I found

Rosa's building anchored by a picturesque restaurant on the ground level, with a mint green awning and outside seating. Luckily, she had mailed me the key to the place, and I found my way into the lobby and counted the forty-seven steps up to the apartment. She told me the name outside the door read "Dimora del Sole," which translated into "sunshine abode" in English. And then I saw the number next to the name. Number 7, Dimora Del Sole. Forty-seven steps to Apartment Number 7. Was this fate? For a moment, I imagined my grandmother smirking at me from heaven. I caught myself grinning at the thought of it.

As I put the key into the door, there seemed to be music coming from inside, and it made me nervous. Did I have the right place? What if I walked in on someone, or worse, on some people, doing, well, whatever it is that people might be doing on a late afternoon in romantic, sunny Italy? Tentatively, I turned the doorknob and pushed the door open.

I had been right, there was music coming from inside the place, so I walked over to the source. Rosa had left a radio on and placed fresh flowers on the kitchen table, along with a note that read "Benvenuta," or "welcome" in Italian. I took off my coat and placed my bags down, as I drooled over the apartment. With high ceilings and crown molding, arched doorways, and terra cotta-colored floors, it had character, and the walls of the apartment were a calming off-white color. The furniture, antiques mixed with more modern fare, was incorporated perfectly, and the living area had a soft, white couch with lots of chairs positioned across from it. The kitchen featured numerous large windows across the back that let in the light.

 The apartment was warm, so I adjusted the heat and cracked the windows to let some fresh air in as the sounds from the streets drifted inside of my new little abode. I loved how Italians didn't have screens on their windows; it made you feel as if you were part of the outdoors without that little barrier. Feeling thirsty, I opened up the refrigerator and found that my aunt had already stocked it with milk, eggs, pastries, and fresh fruits. Fresh bread was wrapped in brown paper and was sitting on the counter. Then, I spotted the homemade red gravy in jars. The cabinets had been filled with an assortment of pasta, as well, and I was thankful for that. I was absolutely famished.

When I took a peek at the bedrooms, and chose the bigger one for myself, I noticed that everything I had shipped from America was already there in the room, stacked in the corner, waiting to be unpacked. Rosa must have had her sons help her transport them here.

I texted Rosa right away, feeling so appreciative. She spoke pretty solid English, so I wrote simply:
Thank you. The place is amazing, and I'm grateful that you brought my things here. It was so nice of you to do this for me. Looking forward to seeing you soon.

Truly exhausted from the day's journey, I ate fresh cheese and bread, boiled up the homemade pasta and red gravy, and drank Pellegrino water that was in my fridge. After ingesting all those delicious carbs, I drifted off on the couch, the reverberations of Siena lulling me fast asleep.

— Chapter 3 —

"You made it," my editor said as I picked up the phone on the second ring in the morning. She had woken me up, but I didn't mind. I'd slept for almost twelve hours, having been up all night on the airplane.

"I made it," I said.

"How's the place?"

"It's lovely, Danielle. Really beautiful. And thanks for the car and driver."

"You're welcome. Take a week to get settled and you can get started on the piece for the website. You know what I want, right?"

"I've got it. I'm on it," I said.

"Okay, great. Well, keep in touch and let me know if you need anything on our end…research or otherwise."

"I will. Thanks, Danielle. And thanks for entrusting Italy to me."

"We all know you're the perfect person to write these stories. Quite frankly, I'm a little jealous," she said.

"Don't be surprised if I show up on your doorstep one day and beg to sleep in the second bedroom."

"Anytime," I said. "You're helping me pay my bills."

I knew I needed to get cracking on the first story. Danielle had shared the idea with me prior to my departure. As a staff writer, my articles appeared in both the printed version of the magazine and the online site, so I often wrote several stories a month.

I showered, stepped into jeans, sweater and my boots, and headed out to stroll the streets. Unpacking could wait. I was in Italy, and I wanted espresso from a coffee shop, just the way Elizabeth Gilbert grabbed one in *Eat, Pray, Love*. I felt a little bit like her at the moment and was excited to do this—ready to explore and write about Italy.

After I took a quick shot, I ordered a black coffee to go along with a sfogliatelle. Back home, you can't get good sfogliatelles, except for one particular pasticerria in the city.

After I received my order, I found a bench outside and took a seat, watching all the early birds pass by. I was always amazed by how many people woke up early and began their days just after the sun had risen. I bit into the sfogliatelle covered in powdered sugar. Bliss. There really wasn't anything in the world like a flaky, sweet, Italian sfogliatelle. *How would I describe the taste of it in a story?* I would have to think about that.

Despite that it was January, the day was mild. *I was here.* A smile crept across my lips. When I traveled for my job, I'd grown accustomed to the days spent by myself exploring, but I always knew I had family and friends to return to when the assignment was over. In my present situation, I would live alone—and would be alone a lot of the time. But in reality, there was an advantage to being by yourself; you made your own schedule, and if you wished to make a fool out of yourself, you could do it without anyone finding out about it on Facebook. Added bonus.

"C'è qualcuno seduto qui?" a man said to me, gesturing to the side of the bench I was not occupying. I surmised he wanted to sit there.

"Sì," I said.

He opened his newspaper and began to look it

over. He glanced at me and smiled as I watched him fold the paper and begin reading the pages. I could parse together the headlines because of my limited vocabulary. When I finished the coffee and pastry, I walked back to Piazza del Campo, which was just around the bend. It truly is one of the most beautiful piazzas in all of Italy. I remembered the stories my mother would share about the Palio horse races when I was little. My mother had been to the races several times. This morning, people were wearing their winter coats, strolling the large square, and businesses on the perimeter were beginning to open.

I walked around the piazza for about an hour until my lower back became cranky from the long plane ride. I really needed to stretch or do yoga.

As I walked back to my place and trudged up the forty-seven steps, I noticed my next-door neighbor picking up his own newspaper outside his door. He was an older man, and he saw me and gave me a wave.

"Ciao," I said.

"Ciao," he said back to me, trying to focus on who I was and if he knew me.

"Sei cugino di Rosa?" he asked. *Are you Rosa's cousin?*

"Sì," I said, "ma non parlo molto bene l'italiano." *Yes—I don't speak good Italian.* "Arrugginita." *Rusty.*

"Ah, ah," the older man said. And then in English, "I speak-a da English."

"Well, yes, you do. Very well!" I said. He laughed. "It is nice to meet you."

"Ah, sì," he said, walking toward me to greet me. "Ah, you be-a happy in Siena?"

"Sì," I said. "Very happy."

"Benvenuta for you," he said, motioning for me to come into his apartment. He walked inside his door, and I followed. Because his apartment is on the corner of the building, I noticed the sunlight streamed in through the windows a little differently from mine, the winter rays lighting the space.

"Vieni a vedere il panorama," he said, testing my Italian language skills and motioning me to come inside and look out his windows, and he grabbed a small bag of Baci chocolates with a bow on them and gave them to me.

"Grazie," I said, pleased at the thoughtful gift.

I walked over, looking around his very neatly kept apartment, colorful paintings on the walls, and marveled at its lack of clutter. The place smelled as if it had just been cleaned.

"Tale bellezza, no?"

"Yes. Bellisimo." His apartment really was beautiful. Right then, I wished I had brushed up on my Italian or taken a Rosetta Stone course prior to coming. He sat down in his chair that faced the window, and motioned me to sit, so I lowered myself into the chair across from him.

The man smiled at me, and I could see that he was probably quite handsome back in the day. His distinguished face was wrinkled with age, but his olive skin caught the light in the best of ways, giving his face a youthful glow. He had thick grey hair, and his cheeks were rosy. Average in stature, he wore trousers with a button-down shirt that looked a little rumpled.

"Is that your wife?" I asked the man.

He picked up the photo and handed it to me. "Sì," he said, pointing up to the sky. "With-a God now."

I nodded. I could tell it was difficult for him to say those words.

"My Nana, too," I said, attempting to share a bond

with the gentleman.

"Così triste..." he said. *Sad*.

"Sì," I said.

He pointed to the deck of cards sitting on the table beside him. Then, he pointed to me and the cards. "You play?"

"Sì," I said.

"We play-a da cards. You a-tell-a me stories about Americano, and I a-teach-a-you a better Italiano."
His English was better than okay, and it made me wonder how he learned. If only I'd given the Italian language the same effort. We made plans to play cards on Wednesday night, and I promised to fill him in on American life. I excused myself and explained that I had to unpack and get settled.

As I put the key in my door and heard him close his, I realized I never even asked him his name.

— Chapter 4 —

Rosa texted me at seven-thirty the next morning. *You come for supper tomorrow night. Alessandro will pick you up.*

After eating toast and having a quick coffee, I strode off in the direction of a market to get some items: fresh fruits, vegetables, and cooking spices.

I bundled up for the walk—the temperatures had dipped overnight—and grabbed my purse and headed out the door.

The sun was shining brightly, and the sky was flawless, one of those crisp winter days. The buildings twinkled in the sunlight, and the terra cotta colors complemented the aqua blue sky.

Winding through the back streets, I made my way to a store—Guiseppi's. It looked like it was primed for a role in a film set here in Italy. The muted slate streets led to his specialty shop with a stone exterior and arched doors lined with vines, and fresh fruits and vegetables graced the sidewalk in barrels and bins. Inside, the shop oozed with charm, as breads and olive oils, pastas of all kinds, and cooking utensils, pots, and pans were displayed around the perimeter of the store.

It smelled delicious in there, too.

"Pronto," the large man with dark hair said to me.

"Pronto," I said back. He smiled.

I grabbed a basket and began to fill it with things I needed for the kitchen—and for my cooking. I had sworn I would learn how to make some of Siena's finest meals, and to learn my way around a kitchen a little bit better. When I had been with Paul, we had cooked together a lot. He was a chef, and he tried to teach me what he learned. If only I'd paid closer attention. Prior to Paul, Ben and I rarely made meals together. We always ate out. In the two years we were together, I could count on my hand the number of times we ate dinner together in his condo, mostly because Ben worked fourteen-hour days in the financial industry, and I was often on the road. The two of them couldn't have been more different, and yet I had loved them both.

And both relationships ended in disaster.

Putting the past out of my mind and reminding

myself that I was, in fact alone, thousands of miles from them both, I couldn't help but feel acutely aware of my singleness. Neither of my previous boyfriends loved me in the way that I had loved them. Neither of them, I realized much later, wanted what I wanted in life. So here I stood, holding a ream of garlic, because frankly, now I could eat as much of it as I liked, and no one would tell me that I reeked of it.

There were certainly pluses to not being in a relationship.

As I brought my basket up to the counter to check out, the man looked at me sideways. I looked back at him, and he smiled. I knew he could tell I was American.

"You know Rosa Vinelli?"

"Sì," I said.

"Ah," he said, coming from around the counter to face me. He caught me off guard by taking my face in his large hands and kissing me on both cheeks. His stubble tickled my skin. "You-a look like her. She told me you were coming. *Famiglia.*"

I smiled at him and nodded. His English was strong behind the Italian accent.

"How long you are-a visiting?"

"Well, I'll be living here for a year," I said. "I'm writing travel articles about Italy for my magazine."

"Bene!" he said. "What is your first story?"

"It's about La Festa Degli Innamorati. What can you tell me about it?" I asked. He seemed interested and chatty, so I figured I'd ask.

"Well, it is a lover's tradition, all about love. All about romance."

"Only for lovers, correct?" I asked him.

"Si, it is not Americanized here-a in Italy. Lovers only."

I thanked him for the information, and when I went to shake his hand, he came from around the counter and kissed it instead. He also gave me everything in the basket at no charge.

*

"You told Guiseppi I was going to his shop," I said to Rosa on the phone after I left.

"I did. I wanted him to know you were stopping

by. You said you were."

"I was supposed to be incognito, you know, scoping the place out."

"In-cog what? You said you were going. I thought you should meet. He's a nice man," Rosa said.

"He was. Very nice man."

"We look forward to having you for dinner with la familia."

"Si," I said.

"Alessandro will pick you up at five. We look forward to seeing your American face."

"Italian now," I told her, and we hung up.

*

I found my way back to the apartment, the cumbersome bag positioned on my hip as I walked up the steps simulating how one would carry a small child and began to climb the forty-seven steps to my place. Feeling suddenly hungry after inhaling scents from the sidewalk restaurants, I reached inside my purse for the key. Propping the bag on one leg, my purse strewn across my shoulder while attempting to insert the key into the lock, I saw a man striding toward me. He looked vaguely familiar.

"You need help?" he asked me, his Italian accent coming through in his almost perfect English words.

"I'm fine, thank you," I said.

"American neighbor."

"Sì – yes."

"You're playing cards with Matteo on Wednesday," he said, a big smile creeping across his face.

I looked at him funny. How did he know so much?

"I'm sorry, I'm Nicolo, Matteo's grandson."

Just then, my neighbor's door opened, and he stepped outside into the hallway. "Nico—Hai dimenticato il portafoglio." Nicolo walked back toward my neighbor and grabbed his wallet, shaking his head at himself.

"Grazie. Arrivederci, Nonno," Nicolo said, embracing my neighbor in a hug.

I smiled at him as he headed for the floor's exit behind me. "Ciao, Anna," he said, as he strolled by me toward the steps.

The older man I now knew as Matteo waved to me,

and I waved back, as I heard the fading sound of Nicolo's shoes as he descended the steps, and it dawned on me that he had already learned my name without me telling him.

– Chapter 5 –

The next day, I received a letter in the mail at Rosa's apartment. I recognized the handwriting right away, but oddly, there was no return address.

Dear Anna,

I am writing this letter a few days before you get on the plane for your new adventure so that you get it soon after you arrive in Italy. I didn't want you to feel too lonely, so I figured a piece of mail from your family each week wouldn't hurt. I can't wait to come visit you. I also thought it might make you look important if you started to receive mail. You know...sort of the "mysterious woman in Siena" receiving mail from a mysterious person in America kind of thing. I will write each week, so that the letters keep arriving and you feel more than loved by your family here.

It wasn't easy to kiss my beloved daughter goodbye and send her off to my childhood stomping grounds, but I know you will enjoy your time in Italy again. Remember how much fun you had when you studied abroad? As you and I talked, you will have time to recharge your batteries.

You're in Siena now. Open your eyes. See the world. Write about it. Drink good wine. Savor the bread. Learn to cook. Hang out with your cousins. Meet new people. Open your heart to the right people.

And enjoy your sabbatical from here for a while.
Just don't get fat. ;-)
I love you, vita mia.
Mom.

I began to choke up reading that letter. I missed my mother already. She had always been my rock—always believing in me, and even when she didn't love the people I dated, she trusted in me. After both of my relationships ended, she simply told me that God put those people in my life for a reason, and that good would come from it all. It was tough to believe when I poured my heart and soul into both relationships, and with Paul it had been over five years. After everything ended with Ben two years ago—and knowing that I wanted a family more than anything in the world—the depression started to get to me. Plus, I couldn't bear to go on one more blind date and disappoint friends who thought they were doing me some good.

When your heart's broken and you're not ready for something new, everything is lackluster. And after two devastating breakups, you began to look in the mirror and wonder what was wrong with you. Neither man could see "forever" with me, and that notion called for some true introspection.

To be honest, I began to see myself as not worthy of a solid, true, loving relationship. My mother told me it was baloney.

"Everyone is loveable, Anna," she had said. But was that true? As Paul had said to me, "I love you, but I'm not in love with you anymore." Words like that can damage your soul. It was amazing I even had it in me to start something new with Ben many, many months after Paul ended our relationship.

Watching me sulk had bothered my mother after a while. I lived only a few miles from her and saw her regularly. We talked on the phone most days. "Pick yourself up by the bootstraps," she had said, "and throw yourself into your work for a while."

I did that. I worked. I traveled. I did exactly as she said and became engrossed in my work so much so that I neglected to have any sort of social life. Hiding became a crutch to cope with the hurt.

To be fair, there were millions of us who walked around with broken hearts. We've lost loved ones to illness; we've found ourselves alone because those we love have fallen out of love with us; and we've lost loved ones who simply no longer care and don't want to be connected with us. I knew I was not the only one—that countless others suffer—and yet being a member of that particular club made it nonetheless lonely, and increasingly sadder by the day. I admired those who genuinely didn't mind the solitude and were happy not to be attached to someone else. There was something so inspiring about that.

I had almost given up believing that I was worthy of a longstanding love relationship. I beat myself up constantly, and my mother was tired of watching me do it.

"Perhaps your time in Italy will help you find the

answers you are looking for. Rosa wants you to come and stay in her place. You have extended family in Siena. And we will come and visit. Go clear your head. Nana would have insisted that you go."

"Would she have? Really?"

"You know how much Nana loved Italy. And she would have loved watching your career blossom as a travel writer. I can hear her in my head, saying, 'Arianna, you get your butt on that plane and heal. Learn to love yourself first, before you love anyone else,'" my mother said.

I scratched my head.

I hated when my mother was right sometimes, but it was absolutely true. Nana would have said that.

*

Alessandro arrived at five o'clock sharp. I was waiting for him on the street just outside the walled city so it would be easy for him to pick me up. I hadn't seen my cousin in fifteen years. He pulled the car over, got out, and hugged me, kissing both sides of my cheeks.

"Anna—so good to see you!" he said.

"You, too, Alessandro. And thank you so much for helping me get set up in the apartment." His dark skin and dark eyes twinkled, and he smelled of a musk cologne.

I climbed inside his little car, and he began to make the drive outside Siena and through the hills. On the ride, Alessandro filled me in on his life: he married a woman from town, and they had a three-year-old daughter, Gianna. I couldn't wait to meet her.

"It has been too long, Anna," he said, as I marveled at the scenery of Tuscany. I'd forgotten its beauty. The hills sloped and the cypress trees graced the hilltops. It was like reading beautiful poetry, and it nearly brought me to tears, the scenery enveloping me, the houses perched like visions of perfection on the landscape.

"It's so gorgeous. I can see why you are so happy here with your family, and why you would never want to leave," I said. He smiled at me and patted my hand.

When we rounded the corner and began the drive up the dirt pathway to their home, the vines still in full bloom and the arbors covered with crawling flowers, I was in awe of the place. Instantly, I was overtaken by the vibrant colors, the smells of the countryside, and the charm of Rosa's house—it epitomized Tuscan splendor.

Just then, Rosa came running out of her house, an apron covering her dress, and embraced me in a hug. "Here she is—welcome! Welcome!" she said, hugging me so tightly into her large bosom I could barely breathe.

Little Gianna stood next to her mother, Alessandro's wife Victoria, and I waved to her. She gave me a timid wave back, probably wondering who this foreign woman was joining them for dinner. I was glad I had worn a dress for the occasion. Rosa was entertaining us in the home's large dining room, with windows all along the back the allowed the hills to be a backdrop. The long dining table was adored with twinkle lights, candles, and flowers. Italian splendor.

"You're too skinny," Rosa said to me. "Are you ready for a feast?"

I laughed. Never in my entire life had I been called skinny. I had hips and curves, and I'd always had to work very hard to maintain my weight. It wasn't easy—because I loved food. My mother even cautioned me not to gain weight. I know she said it lovingly, but she knew I could look at food and put on five pounds. She and I were very similar that way.

"I am ready. This all looks amazing!" I said.

The wine began to pour. I was reunited with my cousins and their children. Rosa's husband, my uncle Pietro, a sophisticated looking man, was warm and welcoming. We passed the numerous plates of food Rosa had prepared around the table. I felt comfortable right away, even though I hadn't seen them all in many years. But Italian families were like that—it was as if no time had passed at all, and we just jumped in right where we left off.

Except, perhaps for Pietro, who wanted to know the details of my love life as soon as I took a bite of the second course.

"So, no marriage prospects then, Anna?"

I almost choked on my food. Italians can be so blunt. They don't hide behind formalities.

"Not at the moment," I said, obviously embarrassed.

Sensing my humiliation, Alessandro saved me. "Papa, she wants to find the perfect person, not a *perdente*."

I looked at him sideways, not understanding the word. "*Loser*," he whispered to me.

Luckily, Pietro let it go at that, and the rest of the meal consisted of us sharing family stories, especially ones about my mother as a child, and I offered a glimpse into our life in the United States. Sitting where I was right now, in the candlelight of this old, Tuscan home, eating savory food, and enjoying my family's company, I'd say I was in the right spot for now.

When I said goodbye to everyone that evening and climbed back in Alessandro's car for the ride back to the city of Siena, I thought about what Alessandro had said to everyone at the table on my behalf: not a *perdente*.

He was so right. This time around, I would not entertain the idea of someone who did not love me the right way...the way I needed to be loved. I wanted someone who said they loved me—all of me—and that they were *in love* with me, not just that they loved me. There was a difference. I was thankful I had decided to take this respite here in Italy, to find a new focus, and regain my self-confidence as well.

— Chapter 6 —

On Tuesday, I spent the day getting my assignments organized. Danielle and I talked on the phone for an hour, lining up my travel within Italy. I was going to Rome, Venice, and Florence, and then to some of the smaller regions and towns. Her assistant booked my hotels for those jaunts.

Luckily, Rosa had packaged leftovers for me for two nights, so I relaxed with a new book I'd picked up and ate dinner. I even poured myself a small glass of wine. After dinner, I needed fresh air and slipped into my coat for a nighttime stroll.

Being alone wasn't so bad, after all. I got to do whatever I wanted and was on my own timetable. I ate what I wanted when I wanted; I took walks when it suited my own schedule; I had plenty of time to read; and I even took time for meditation in the mornings and before bed. "Find yourself," my mother had said to me. I wanted her to know I had listened. I was doing what I said I would do.

Wednesday morning was much the same: I got up, had breakfast, and began to do research for my first article. Tonight, I had a date to play cards with my neighbor, Matteo. I was looking forward to getting to know him better.

To that end, I bought desserts from my local pasticceria and a plant for Matteo. He seemed like a sweet man who had lost his wife, and I was looking forward to his company. It also was unlikely that I'd be any good at cards.

Not wanting to be late, I knocked on the door a couple of minutes early.

"Ah, princepessa, so good to see you," Nicolo said, with a smile. He was wearing a crisp, maroon shirt and his glasses. He looked very smart and tidy, and he caught me off-guard, as I was not expecting him to be joining us. Nicolo saw my surprise. "I always play cards with him on Wednesdays. He must have forgotten to mention that."

He motioned dramatically for me to come inside, and I saw Matteo sitting at the card table, ready to play.

Music featuring an accordion played in the background, and I could see Matteo shuffling the cards.

"Come in, come in," he said. "Ah, Anna," Matteo said when he saw me enter the room. "Ciao, bella. We are happy you come."

"Grazie."

I presented Matteo with the plant, and he took the desserts from me from the pasticerria.

"Eccelente!" He looked pleased by the sweet treats. "Sit, sit," Matteo said. "We play da cards."

"Which game?" I asked.

"We play Scopa. You know how?"

"Of course, she knows how! You do, don't you, Anna?" Nicolo asked.

I smiled. "Yes—si—my grandmother taught me," I said.

Matteo nodded and smiled once he understood. Nicolo watched me as I made myself at home at the table.

And there I was. Sitting in my neighbor's apartment playing cards with an older gentleman and his grandson, his younger clone. It was uncanny how much they looked alike. There was something in the twinkle of their eyes that made it clear they were not only related by blood but connected in a much deeper way. My sixth sense was kicking in—and I could feel that. I think it's one of the reasons I enjoyed writing and hearing people say they connected with my travel pieces.   While it's always about the places we visit, underlying all of that is the people—the people who make up the place. Additionally, people always told me I looked like my grandmother more than I looked like my own mother—perhaps it was the hazel green eyes and the shape of our faces—but everyone knew I looked like Nana. The same was true for Nicolo and Matteo; they both had strong Roman noses.

"So, how are you enjoying Siena?" Nicolo asked me.

"Good." Then I asked, as I am always curious to know more, "Nicolo, how do you speak English so well?"

"At school. We learned Italian and English."

It made me wish I were truly bilingual. The desire to work on my Italian was growing exponentially as I began to become reacquainted with the culture.

After about fifteen minutes, Matteo won the first round. He clearly was a little devil at playing Scopa.

Nana had told me years ago that it was the favorite card game of the older gentlemen in Italy. If Matteo was any indication of their love of the game, I knew I was going to lose at cards all night.

"So, how long will you be with us, Anna?" Nicolo asked.

"I'll be working here for a year."

"What do you do?"

"I'm a travel writer."

"What a great job. Sounds delightful," he said.

"It is pretty nice. I love to write and don't mind the travel."

I could see Matteo's ears perk up when he heard Nicolo and me talk about what I do for a living.

"What is your first assignment?" Nicolo asked.

"It's about La Festa Degli Innamorati," I said. Matteo looked at me quizzically. "I have to get started on it, and I've been doing some research. But I could use some more inspiration. Do either of you have a good story about Valentine's Day here in Siena?"

They thought for a moment, and Nicolo yielded to Matteo, who said, "A Siena l'ispirazione è tutt'intorno a te." Matteo had been following along perfectly and replied back to me in English—*In Siena, inspiration is all around you.*

We played another hand, and Matteo won again. His eyes danced with enjoyment.

"He loves winning," Nicolo said.

"I see that. How often do you spend time together?"

"I come by at least three times a week. I try to get him out, too. We go to dinner or to hear music. But always cards on Wednesday nights when I'm not working."

"And what do you do for a living?" I asked Nicolo.

"I'm a travel writer," he said.

"Are you serious? Really?" I could hear Matteo snicker. He was enjoying this conversation.

"No, I'm only joking you," Nicolo said. "I'm a doctor. Pediatra."

"A pediatrician? Here in Siena?"

"Yes. Just around the corner."

"Si prende cura di me," Matteo said. *He takes good care of me.*

"Matteo, why are you speaking to me in Italian if you know English so well."

"Ti sto insegnando l'italiano," he said. *I'm teaching you Italian.*

I should have known. Clever old dog. But I was even more impressed with Nicolo being a doctor and taking care of children.

We ate a bit of the sweets, played one more round, and then when I could see Matteo was beginning to tire, we began to clean up. Matteo put the plant I gave him on the windowsill and settled into his easy chair, turning on the television to watch his favorite news program.

"This was fun, even though I'll never beat Matteo at cards," I said to Nicolo in the kitchen as we put the food and drinks away. "I'm glad he invited me to come over."

"I am glad you came, too," Nicolo said. "He hasn't been the same since Nonna died. He misses her big." *Big.* Good choice of words. I missed my Nana big, too.

"How long were they married?" I asked.

"Fifty-five years."

"That's a long time," I said, in awe.

"And in love with each other all those years—and still—as you can see. All of the paintings in the apartment are Nonna's. She was quite an artist."

"I'll have to take a close look at them sometime," I said.

"His heart, it is always broken," Nicolo said. "It makes me sad to see him this way. I come around to help and to cheer him up as much as I can. But he's lonely."

"Well, I will keep a good eye on him, too. I can care for him, also."

"I appreciate that, Anna. Could I possibly get your mobile number, just in case? He doesn't always answer the phone, and my parents are no longer living in Siena. They moved to the coast, so they've left Nonno, who refused to go with them, in my care. Which I don't mind at all. He's my Nonno."

"Of course," I said, and Nicolo and I exchanged our contact information.

I walked back into the living area and leaned down to meet Matteo's eyes. "*Grazie per la bella serata, anche se mi hai battuto a carte.*" *Thank you for a lovely evening, even though you beat me in cards.* I kissed Matteo on the cheek.

"*Nessun problema,*" Matteo said, laughing. *No problem.*

"I will see you tomorrow," I said to them both.
Nicolo walked me to the door.
"Ciao, bella," he said.

– Chapter 7 –

A week later, as I was eating supper, and after another week of playing cards and losing to both Matteo and Nicolo, the light of the day coming to an end, I heard a knock on my door.

Matteo stood before me with an old, leather tattered box that looked worn. It was a pretty sizeable one, and it was tied shut with a big ribbon.

"That looks heavy," I said, taking it from him and carrying it inside. "Come on in." We moved into the living area, where he sat on one of the guest chairs, and I placed the box on the coffee table.

"What is this?"

"Stoooria d'amore." *A love story.*

I looked at him a bit puzzled.

"My eyes are bad, and my hands no work the typewriter like they used to. It is storia d'amore I have-a worked on for years. My-a story. Our-a story. Lenora and I."

"May I?" I asked him, pointing to the box.

"Sì."

I opened the box and saw faded letters tied up in ribbons, black and white and color photographs, handwritten poetry, and a stack of typewritten pages tied up with string. In awe, I looked at the contents of the box. It was a reservoir of documentation, a scribe's scrawling on paper here and there, bits and pieces of stories everywhere. Cards in red envelopes.

"When did you stop writing this?"

"Five-a years ago when Lenora pass."

"Matteo—were you a writer?"

"Giornalista." Journalist.

"Really?" I asked. He nodded.

Looking at some of the photographs was like looking at Nicolo. Their similarities were striking, and Lenora reminded me of Nana when she was younger—voluptuous with sweet eyes and an angelic smile. In photo after photo, you could see how much in love Matteo and Lenora were.

Danielle had wanted a unique piece about love and

Valentine's Day for the website—a more personal story, if I could find one.

As I perused the collection, aspects of their love story unfolded here in this box, but would I be able to tell this story? I could, I thought. Matteo is here to help fill in the blanks. Was I holding the key to an untold love story—one that I could sink my teeth into? Dissecting the contents of the box was like being handed the parts of a car before it's put together, and I understood what he wanted me to do.

"Thank you for sharing this with me," I said.

"It's-a yours," he said.

"I can't keep this—these are all your treasures."

"You write the story on La Festa Degli Innamorati. On-a loan. Here is-a your ispirazione for your story."

"Are you sure, Matteo? I would be reading these private letters and poetry—"

"It is all there to be a-read. It is good story, a nice story, and we need a little nice in this world. Spread the love."

I couldn't argue with him. Kindness is always important in life, to any story. And I was intent on doing just as he said—spreading Italy's love.

My heart was filled with gratitude that this man would entrust his love story to me. I had come to Italy to find myself, to get away from it all, but in reality, I had found something that made my heart sing. And maybe his, too.

"And you will help me fill in the blanks?"

"I will-a help you," he said.

— Chapter 8 —

    Fate sometimes has a funny way of finding you. I'd never much believed in fate before, or the luck of Nana's superstitious number seven. I'd never seen luck lean in my direction. But for the first time in many years, I felt differently about fate. Perhaps fate and I had the potential to forge a friendship.

    Matteo's collection was filled with love. It was an ode to his life with Lenora, and while it's an unlikely proposition to glean an entire love story from a lifetime of handwritten notes, love letters, poetry, and withered photographs, sometimes it can be just enough to get the story moving. I also began to type up notes and questions in my computer—things I wanted to ask Matteo to help fill in the gaps. I'd never tackled anything like this before.

    Fate. The official definition of the word, according to Merriam Webster is this: *the will or principle or determining cause by which things in general are believed to come to be as they are or events to happen as they do: destiny.*

After speaking with Matteo, I realized why he had handed me the box. Matteo and Lenora met on La Festa Degli Innamorati by happenstance. The hook of a true Valentine's story had landed in my lap. It was fate. Lenora's friend had asked her to watch her little brother while she snuck out to see a boy her parents did not like. Matteo had brought the brother's bicycle back to him after leaving it at his parents' shop. Their meeting was not planned, nor was it intended, and when the two met face-to-face for the first time, it was love at first sight.

As I interviewed Matteo one afternoon in his apartment over a glass of wine and some cheese and grapes, I became more intrigued by their stories. Call it a modern-day *Romeo and Juliet*, Lenora's parents were not too fond of Matteo. They were protective of their daughter, and they weren't sure Matteo came from the type of background they wished for their daughter. His family had little money, but he worked hard, and was an avid reader, and when he got his first job in his teens at a local newspaper, he started as the errand boy and worked his way up through the ranks to become a journalist. He had to travel a lot, and their clandestine relationship stayed strong during their time apart.

Matteo was a romantic man. I listened as he told me stories in broken English and I asked questions to clarify. When the two finally came clean and told their parents they were madly in love, Lenora's parents were no longer upset. In their eyes, Matteo had worked hard both at his profession and to keep her happy to earn their daughter's love.

I watched as Matteo told me story after story. He loved her so wholeheartedly, I'd never been this close to witnessing such a perfect love. I was falling in love with Matteo's sense of how a relationship should be.

Feverishly making notes, I heard the key enter the lock of Matteo's front door.

"Nicolo," Matteo said to me.

The day had escaped me. In the morning, I began writing a piece on Siena for the print version of the magazine, and all afternoon I had spent with Matteo. This story was slated to be the headline Valentine's story for the website that Danielle was expecting. I wanted to get it just right.

"Why are you two still working? It's time for cards," he said, as he moved to the kitchen and began to put a bag of groceries away. I looked at the clock and couldn't believe how engrossed I had become in the work I was doing.

I walked into the kitchen to see if Nicolo needed any help. "I'm so sorry—we've been—"

"When are you going to interview me for the book?" Nicolo asked. "I have some things to say about Romeo and Nonna."

I smiled. "I will. Theirs is quite a love story."

"It is, isn't it? Something to aspire to, no?"

"Si," I said.

"Come," Nicolo said. "Matteo waits for you. I'm not sure if it's documented in that box of stuff, but the truth is, he may be patient in love, but he is not a patient man when it comes to cards."

*

Rosa called me the next morning.

"There is someone we want you to meet. One of

Alessandro's friends. He is nice."

Rosa called everyone nice, so I was skeptical.

"Are you trying to play matchmaker?"

"Well, if you are lonely. Italy is a place for love, Arianna." She was the only one in the family who called me by my full name. Everyone else called me Anna.

"I'm not lonely. I have lots of things that keep me occupied. I'm on deadline to write a story—about love."

"So maybe you need some love?"

"It's not about me," I told her. She was incorrigible.

I video chatted with my mother after that. I needed to talk with her about everything that was happening.

"There you are—you're looking so well!" my mother said.

"Thank you. It doesn't hurt that I like to take long evening walks, even in the cold. I had forgotten how beautiful Siena is. And Rosa's villa. It's just stunning. I can't wait to see it with the gardens in bloom in the summer."

"I know. I miss it."

"When are you coming to visit?" I asked her.

"Soon, I promise. So what's going on?"

"Rosa wants to set me up with one of Alessandro's friends."

"Are you not up to it?"

"I don't know. I just don't know. I like how it is right now."

"Well, you know what they say—there's no harm in meeting him."

I supposed she was right. I couldn't lock myself away from life, from trying again. I didn't have to sacrifice anything but my time, and so with encouragement from my mother, I agreed to meet Alessandro's friend. What harm could it do?

*

As I stared at myself in the full-length mirror unhappy with the simple black dress I'd chosen to wear to dinner and wishing I had bought something new, I heard a knock on my door. My date was almost a half an hour early.

"Coming," I said.

I opened the door, and to my surprise, it was not

my date, but Nicolo.

"You look bellisimo," he said.

"Thank you," I said. "What's up? We don't have cards tonight, do we?"

"No," Nicolo said. "I was just stopping by and didn't know if you wanted to go to dinner with Matteo and me. I'm getting him out of the house."

"Oh, I wish I could. I have a —"

"Date?"

"A set up date by my aunt."

"Oh," Nicolo said. "Well, let us not interrupt you. Have a good time."

"Thanks—I'll see you next week," I said. "Or sooner—I need to interview you for the piece about your grandparents."

"Call me," he said, walking toward Matteo's door.

*

An hour later, my date texted me and asked me to meet at the restaurant, as he was running late from his job. When I arrived at the door of the restaurant and saw him, I swallowed hard. Dominic may have been the most handsome man I've ever laid eyes upon. He looked like a movie star—tall, lean, tan, with dark hair that looked as if it had been windblown into that exact position and would not move under any circumstances.

As I walked inside the restaurant, the wind from outside caught my skirt and lifted it a little, baring my backside. I pushed it back down and blushed. He laughed and escorted me to our table, pulled out my chair, and we began to talk like two adults who were getting to know one another.

To be fair, he had all the manners and moves any woman would want, albeit perhaps a little self-absorbed. After we ordered and lingered for hours over our food and wine, he told stories about his job in food sales. As I sized him up during the course of the night, by all accounts, he was a catch.

But my heart felt nothing. Nothing. It did not skip any beats and there were moments during the evening when he discussed his job and I had to suppress a yawn. It almost made me panic, as if I should go check my pulse in the ladies' room. He wasn't a bad guy; I just didn't feel chemistry whatsoever.

After dinner, he insisted on walking me back to my place.

"I hope you had a nice night," he said to me, as he brushed back a strand of hair from my eyes.

"It was a lovely night. I'm glad Alessandro wanted us to meet. It will be nice to have another friend here in Siena."

"Ah, I see—amica." *Friend.*

I nodded. "You are lovely, Dominic. I am just not ready—for a relationship."

After I said that, I realized that maybe he wasn't interested in one, either. Maybe Dominic was out for fun and not for a relationship at all. There was something about his body language that told the story of a man who was out for a good time, but I knew in my gut that it was going to end at the door. I wasn't going to do that to myself, even if it had been a while. A long, freaking while. Was I dead inside?

He kissed my hand and wished me a good night, and I turned to enter the building and trudged up the forty-seven steps feeling my wrist for any sort of heartbeat.

I turned the corner and bumped straight into Nicolo, who was leaving Matteo's.

"Back already?"

"Yes. What are you still doing here?"

"Truthfully, I fell asleep on Matteo's couch. How was the date?"

"Nice."

"Nice?"

"He was nice, but not for me. Are you going home now?" I asked Nicolo.

"I was. I'm seeing patients very early tomorrow morning. Why?"

"No worries," I said.

"No, what is it?"

"Do you have fifteen minutes to tell me more about Matteo and Lenora? My deadline is looming."

"Sure," he said, and I opened the door to let him in.

— Chapter 9 —

I asked Nicolo if he would like a glass of wine, and he accepted. I'd bought a bottle on the way home the other night and wanted to try it. I liked the packaging of it. It looked like what I thought romance would look like if it were a wine. Perfect. A red label with gold lamé. Sumptuous.

I poured our glasses, and we sat adjacent to each other, making idle chit-chat about Matteo and cards and the weather. I reached for my laptop and opened it, ready to take notes.

"Are you ready?" I asked him.

"Ready."

"Do you have vivid memories of your grandparents as romantics?"

"Yes. All the way up to Nonna's death. Together, they were always smiling and laughing, always kind to one another. They lifted each other up and they were always there for each other. It was the everyday things, both small and big, but mostly small."

I typed his answer.

"Did you know that they met on Valentine's Day, or as you call it here in Italy, La Festa Degli Innamorati."

"He has told that story for many, many years. Always about February 14. Always about love and finding your special someone. My Nonna always said fourteen was her lucky number, because it was the date she met Nonno."

I smiled. There was no way I could hide a smile from creeping across my face.

"Is that funny?" Nicolo asked.

"No," I said. "Well, yes, actually."

"Why?"

"Because my Nana always said the number seven was her lucky number. Everything good that happened to her included the number seven. At least, that was her story."

Nicolo smirked. "And the truth of these stories sometimes becomes blurry, right?"

"What do you mean?"

"I mean, people often embellish their stories to make them sound better, more *drammatico*...to make them more entertaining. Sometimes it's hard to tell the fact from fiction."

"Are you suggesting my grandmother was a liar?"

Nicolo had struck a nerve.

"No, you misunderstand. It's just, as a writer, don't you notice that people tend to make stories try to sound more impressive than they actually are?" He was defending what he had said, trying to justify it.

I took Nicolo's assertion as a slight and wondered if he was questioning the ethics of my storytelling and reporting, of my career as a writer. I didn't embellish anything. I told stories, either from my experience, or from the experiences of others. Was he suggesting I just added to them to make them sound better? My college journalism professor would have had my head on a platter if I compromised my journalistic integrity, though I'm not sure all journalists these days give honesty and integrity any clout. So, there was that.

"I'm honestly not sure what you're suggesting. Are you trying to say that the stories I write are phonies, made up, or that I add to them to give them more substance?"

"No, no, you misunderstand."

"Do I?" I asked. "You're questioning my ethics as a writer."

"No, Anna, you—"

I closed my laptop and put up my hand as a nonverbal cue for him to stop talking. "You know what, Nicolo, I am super tired and on edge with this deadline. We probably should have scheduled this conversation for another time."

He looked gutted by what I just said, and appalled at the way I dismissed him, the words freely pouring out of my mouth.

"If that is what you want," he said. "Fine." And with that, he placed his wine glass on the coffee table, got up out of his chair, walked to the door, and let himself out.

My heart was racing now.

Now I had a pulse.

— Chapter 10 —

When I awakened in the morning, feeling the effects of too much wine over the course of the previous evening with Dominic, I felt badly about having behaved the way I did with Nicolo, not truly realizing the effects of the alcohol I had consumed at dinner. Nicolo and I got off to such a great start, and we'd been playing cards for three weeks now. We had become fast friends, and Matteo was one of the sweetest men I'd ever met. I hoped Nicolo didn't tell Matteo about my bad behavior.

Truthfully, I couldn't exactly put my finger on what made me so sensitive and offended.

Maybe I was premenstrual. That was it. Of course. I could blame it on that. I was about to get my period. I found it quite convenient to use the looming monthly cycle as a scapegoat. It proved handy, even if it wasn't entirely true.

My phone rang, and I jumped. *If it's Nicolo*, I

thought, *I will apologize right away.* I shouldn't have been so assumptive and rude. I felt so ashamed, I wanted to crawl into bed and hide away for the day. But it was Wednesday, and that meant it was cards night. Would I have to cancel with Matteo?

"Hi Danielle," I said, clearing my throat and trying to hide the disappointment in my voice when I saw her number pop up on my screen.

"How's it going? Are you going to have something to me by Tuesday afternoon?"

"I am," I said. "I'm pretty close...and getting closer each minute." A little fib. No one would know. *What just happened to my ethical code? Blaming my cycle for my bad behavior, and now this. My mother would be so disappointed.*

"Great. Well, I'll let you get to it. Just let me know when you send it over."

"Sure thing," I said.

I hung up, and curled up on the sofa for a moment, feeling utterly alone. I wanted to call my mother, but it was the middle of the night their time. I couldn't do that to her.

In my mind, I could hear the words Paul said to me,

and they struck a nerve: *I love you, but I'm not in love with you.* No wonder he said that to me. Was I still harboring hurt feelings regarding my past relationships, and I took that frustration out on Nicolo? On Nicolo—a kind man who takes care of children as a doctor and takes care of his grandfather. I shuddered at the thought of making him so angry that he walked away. He was such a nice guy. He and Matteo had become my first friends here for the last three weeks, and I acted like a buffoon.

There had to be a way to handle the situation before I would see him for the Wednesday card game. I could call him. Or I could apologize to him tonight when I would see him. Or, and I knew it was a bad idea, I could ignore the whole thing altogether. I paced back and forth in the apartment, brewed my coffee, and decided that the first choice was the best one.

I would call and apologize straight away. I was a grown up.

"Siri, call Nicolo," I said.

The phone dialed, and the number rang and rang until it went to voicemail.

My heart sunk, and I made the choice to leave a

message when I heard Nicolo's voice say to do so in Italian.

"Hi, Nicolo, it's Anna. I'm so sorry about last night. I acted, well, I acted stupid. I hope you will forgive me. I would still love to talk with you about Matteo and Lenora before my Tuesday deadline. Please give me a call."

That wasn't so bad, if not humiliating. I had left the message, and now I could concentrate on writing the rest of the story, minus the little parts I needed.

And what I needed was to interview Matteo again and ask him some more questions.

*

"When you and Lenora first met on Valentine's Day, did you feel it was love at first sight?"

"I saw her, and I knew."

"Right away?" I asked.

"Subito." *Immediately.*

I wrote it down.

"And fourteen was her lucky number after that?"

"Per sempre," he said. *Forever. Always.*

In between the short answers, Matteo was able to describe for me their passion for each other, and a couple of times, I actually blushed. Not that he divulged anything about their sex life or any details like that, but he spoke about her so vibrantly and intimately, that I felt my face become warm. The way he talked about Lenora, or more specifically, the way he loved her so deeply, made me question my own relationships: had I ever felt that type of love before? I thought I had, but perhaps I hadn't. Or was this kind of love only possible for certain people, and the rest of us just got a less intense version of love?

I envied Matteo. I truly did. After he became lovestruck and he won over her parents, he married Lenora. They had two children and five grandchildren. They had created a picture-perfect life together, despite his travels as a journalist. She worked as a seamstress making wedding gowns, a very profitable business, and she stayed home and raised the children. Matteo was sent all over the world covering foreign affairs as a correspondent for his Italian newspaper. Which explains quite clearly why he spoke English so well.

"Did you and Lenora have any special traditions for La Festa Degli Innamorati?" I asked him.

"Yes. We always write poetry to each other. The ones in the box."

"Those were for La Festa Degli Innamorati?"

He nodded. "We were not-a so-a good poets, but we tried. And it was the thought of it, si?"

"Si," I said. *The thought of it.*

I'd never written a poem for anyone, and I'd never received a poem—and I'm a writer. What the hell was wrong with me? Why had I been settling all those years for men who wouldn't write me poetry? And I didn't even know I wanted someone to write a poem for me until just now.

Matteo must have seen the look of sheer bewilderment on my face and asked me if I needed some water. "No, no, I'm fine, Matteo."

Not only was I lying for the second time in a day—blowing my moral code once again—but I also realized I hadn't heard from Nicolo, and it was admittedly making me a little crazy. It was four o'clock, and I would be seeing him shortly when we all met to play cards.

I spent another half an hour with Matteo, jotting down the answers to all of my questions, before excusing myself to go back to my apartment and freshen up and get something to eat. At this hour, I supposed Nicolo and I were just going to meet face-to-face, and I would apologize then.

*

When I knocked on Matteo's door at seven o'clock, it was Matteo who answered and not Nicolo, as usual.

"Come in, come in," he said to me. He had pretty good mobility and was agile, though he leaned slightly forward when he walked. He caught me looking around the apartment for Nicolo. "No-a Nicolo tonight," Matteo said. "He's busy at work—the night shift."

I had no reason to believe Matteo was violating *his moral code*. I knew he was telling the truth, but admittedly, my confidence dropped a few notches when he said it.

Therefore, that night, Matteo and I played cards without Nicolo. We talked about Italy and Siena, and he told me about the story of Luccheti d'Amore, or the Padlocks of Love that began to spring up all over Italy in 2006. I remembered seeing a news story in America about lovers who wrote their names on a padlock and then threw away the key, which confirmed the lovers' dedication to their relationship. It had become a tradition, although many of the fences and structures were becoming damaged by the weight of the locks. Some railings had to be relocated in Rome. And in Florence, a city known for its Renaissance art, and a place that is not as sentimental about such trivial things, they took them down.

"Lenora and I have a lock. Do you want to see a picture?" he asked.

He walked over to the bookcase and pulled out an album. He put on his readers to see better and leafed through the pages until he found the photograph.
There, on one particular page, was a color picture of Matteo and Lenora taken by a stranger at a gate where they had secured their padlock. The photograph was taken ten months before she died, and it was the last Valentine's Day they had spent together before she passed.

"I wonder if it's still there," he said.

"Have you not gone back to check?"

"È troppo difficile per me." *It's too hard for me.*

I paused, understanding that it would make him melancholy.

"Where exactly is the lock, Matteo?" I asked.

"In Palazzo Piccolomini near the Church of San Martino."

This gave me an idea.

An idea for the story I needed to complete by Tuesday.

— Chapter 11 —

After doing a little morning yoga and eating lunch, depressed that I most likely ruined a perfectly good friendship with Nicolo, I dressed, grabbed my camera, and began the walk to Palazzo Piccolomini. I wanted to walk and stroll in and out of all the side streets and nooks and crannies. The lock was most likely still there, unless, as Matteo had described, they cut them down or relocated them. I had snapped a photo on my phone of Matteo's picture to help guide me. It was like finding a treasure, and I enjoyed the hunt.

I loved walking in Siena. The lack of cars made it pleasant. The air was crisp, but not too terribly cold, and the sun broke away from the clouds. In and out of the streets I walked, until I smelled coffee coming from a shop, and I stopped in for a cup.

I looked at the picture and wondered where this could be? Matteo had a hard time describing the exact street; I'm not sure if his memory could recall it or if he tried not to dwell on it because it made him too sad. Either way, I was a reporter—albeit a travel writer—but I still had a little bit of investigative reporting inside me. When I first began writing for a local newspaper, I covered the crime beat. One always had to wear an investigation hat when covering that subject. Perhaps I could conjure up that spirit to find Matteo and Lenora's lock.

From the angle of the photo, I could tell the gate sat atop a hill, in what seemed to be all residential homes on a steep street. People had secured their locks to it, and I could see Matteo's and Lenora's was at the bottom all the way on the left.

After walking in out of streets for about a half hour, I turned a corner and saw the wrought iron gate. It looked just like the one in the photograph. My heart began to pound, and my footsteps quickened. I was anxious to see if I could find the padlock. Standing before it, I scanned the bottom and all the way to the left. It was weighed down by many other locks that had been adhered to the gate. I began to try to lift the locks that had covered the one I believed to be Matteo and Lenora's.

And then, I saw their names.

Matteo + Lenora.

Like two school kids in love, they had secured their padlock to the gate. Like two young lovers who had just found each other and fallen deeply in love, only they had locked up their love decades ago. This was just one small example of their devotion to each other and proved that people had the potential to be romantic in their seventies and beyond. Still in love.

Still madly in love.

This was a story worth telling about La Festa Degli Innamorati.

Italy's the most romantic place on the planet, and Matteo and Lenora's story told the truth about true love, perseverance, and loving someone for a lifetime. It was not a fleeting love. It was not just physical love or mental love. Their love encompassed it all—the big picture of what it means to love someone for the duration of your life.

I stood there taking photographs of the gate and of Matteo and Lenora's lock for a while, knowing it would enhance the story and be an important visual to add to it.

Matteo had also granted permission for us to use several of his photographs. My heart leapt at the idea of what this story was turning into and becoming.

All these people may have fastened padlocks to this gate and thrown away the key, but I knew I had the key to a perfect story for our readers.

*

As I hurried back to my apartment, ready to finish up the story, the clouds began to fill the sky, and I could tell it was going to rain. I hadn't brought an umbrella with me, so I tucked my camera into my camera bag and began to run as fast as I could through the streets. I'm not a fast runner, certainly not fast enough to outrun a rainstorm, and before I knew it the weather gods began to cry. Rain puddles formed in the streets.

Soaking wet, I stopped under a restaurant awning to try to stay dry. It was February, and the rain was cold, but more than that, I didn't want my Nikon to get wet. We always tend to think of places and scenery as beautiful in the sunshine or in the summer months, when the skies are blue and the flowers are in bloom.

Siena was spectacular in the rain.

The pavement glistened and the raindrops echoed off the streets. People scurried about carrying umbrellas, and I remembered the words my mother had written in her letter: *You're in Siena now. Open your eyes. See the world. Write about it. Drink good wine. Learn to cook. Hang out with your cousins. Meet new people. Open your heart to the right people.*

I reached inside the camera bag and pulled out my camera. I wanted to remember this moment. Scanning the scene, I snapped several photos before the server asked me if I'd like to be seated at a table.

"Si," I said. "Mi piacerebbe molto." *I'd like that very much.*

For the next hour and a half, I had a glass of wine, ended up talking to the people who sat at the table next to me, and then searched Google for the perfect recipe for tonight. I had promised myself I'd learn to cook.

As only a promise to yourself and a gut feeling can remind you, the time was now.

*

Before dinner, I uploaded the photos of Matteo and Lenora's padlock onto my computer. I wanted to show Matteo that it was still there—I couldn't wait to show him it was still there.

I knocked on Matteo's door, but there was no answer. I knocked again. No answer.

Disappointed, I turned to walk back to my apartment, when I saw Nicolo come from the stairwell.

My heart skipped a beat. *Wait, what was that feeling in my chest?*

"Ciao," I said.

"Ciao." He stopped at my door and looked at me from behind his glasses.

"Nicolo, I'm sorry I snapped at you."

"It's okay," he said.

"No, it's not. I shouldn't have done that. I'm really sorry for my behavior."

"It's not a problem."

"You're being kind. You're always kind. You and Matteo have both welcomed me so warmly—I'm sorry and ashamed."

He patted me on the shoulder. "It's okay, Anna.

We all have bad days. I have to check on Matteo now."

"I just knocked on his door, and he didn't answer," I said, starting to feel a little alarmed by that.

"Just now?" he asked.

"Yes."

Nicolo reached into his pocket and pulled out the key. He ran to Matteo's door to open it, and I found myself following behind, concerned that something was really wrong.

"Nonno!" Nicolo yelled.

He began looking around the apartment and checking the kitchen, bedrooms, and bathroom. There was no sign of Matteo.

"Where is he?" I asked.

"Wait, what day is it? I've lost track, I've been working so much."

"It's Thursday."

"Oh. Thursdays he sees his friends and then eats at Angelo's house. I forgot about that. Lots of late nights working lately has me all confused."

The two of us began to collect ourselves, laughing a little at how we had panicked.

"Well, I'm glad that he's okay. That was scary."

"I think my lack of food and sleep is getting to me," Nicolo said.

"Well, if you haven't eaten, would you like to eat with me? I'd like to make up for my bad behavior. I'm going to try something new tonight. I promised myself I would learn to cook new Italian recipes."

"Well, that would be nice."

"Yes?" I said.

"Si," he said. "And I can also check on Nonno when he gets home, which will make me feel better."

"Me, too."

— Chapter 12 —

As I had sipped wine earlier that afternoon and ate a first course while waiting for the rain to subside, I had found a Tuscan website with a recipe for chicken and ham involtini, and it looked like something I wanted to try. I had stopped at the market when the weather cleared and bought all the ingredients needed to make the dish.

Nicolo stayed with me in the kitchen as I cooked, and he helped me prepare the food. I poured two glasses of wine, and I began to tell him about the progress of my article and how I had found Matteo's padlock. In between following the directions, I showed Nicolo the pictures on my computer I had uploaded.

"Wow," he said. "That's amazing. I didn't know about that." I could see his eyes become watery and understood how touching this was to see it. I had felt the same way about it after hearing Matteo's story.

"Love lives on even after death. I find that

remarkable," I said.

"Remarkable," he said.

"I can't wait to have a finished piece to show my editor. I hope she will like what I have written."

"I am sure it will be wonderful."

We set the table and lit two candles. I even dimmed the lights. This was the first time I was entertaining in the apartment, and it felt comfortable having Nicolo there. Everything about Nicolo felt comfortable. He felt like home to me, and I realized that perhaps I had been drawn to him without even realizing it. From the moment we met, everything was so easy—until I threw a wrench into it. And while I had become used to living alone in Italy for the last month, it felt so good to deviate from that cycle and be entertaining in the apartment.

"This is delicious—you did a good job making this," Nicolo said. "Tastes like it came from an Italian chef."

"It did," I teased. "I'm Italian, and I made it, so I guess what you're saying is true."

He laughed, and the lightness of the moment, the candlelight, and the wine, put us both into some sort of trance, and as naturally as our friendship began, we leaned toward each other and kissed at the table.

Embarrassed and awkward at first, we both pulled away gently still looking into each other's eyes, and I started to get up from the table and clear the dishes.

"No, wait," he said, reaching for my arm and pulling me closer to him.

He guided me onto his lap and took my face in both of his hands. I removed his glasses and stared into his handsome, chiseled face and wanted to kiss his sweet, soft lips again. This time, there was no awkwardness, only the warm, tingling feeling that went from my lips throughout my body. A sense of longing I hadn't felt in a long time—of desire, and perhaps, care and passion—took hold, and the two of us remained intertwined for minutes.

Suddenly, we heard a knock at the door.

We straightened ourselves up, and I walked toward the door to answer it. Matteo stood before me holding a bouquet of flowers.

"Hi, Matteo. We were worried about you. Glad you are back."

"I always go with a-Angelo on Thursdays. Nicolo, I saw your bicycle out-a front, so I thought I knock."

"Thanks, Nonno," Nicolo said, standing slightly behind me. "Hai comprato dei fiori per Anna?" *You bought flowers for Anna?*

"No, stupido, le ho comprate perché tu le dessi," he said, a little grin forming on his lips. *No, stupid, I bought them for you to give to her.* He handed Nicolo the flowers and gave me a wink. Sly devil.

As he walked away, we heard him whistling a tune. Then he turned to wave and said, "Ciao, bambini," as he stepped inside his apartment and left us to pick up right where we left off.

— Chapter 13 —

I beat my deadline. Inspired by everything I had learned over the last couple of weeks, I had the entire story written and turned into Danielle earlier than she expected. I finished writing and editing it on Sunday night, and Danielle had the piece published on the magazine's website prior to Valentine's Day, with all of the photographs I had provided.

I logged onto the website.

A Lock on Love: The Enduring Love of an Italian Couple, written by Arianna Ricci, published on February 7.

Nana would have been so proud.

Matteo had not wanted to read the piece until it was published. It was the journalist in him. He wanted to see the story come to fruition—the final product—and I wanted to make him proud of me. Neither Matteo nor Nicolo had ever read any of my articles, so this article would be the first.

I watched their eyes and their expressions as both Matteo and Nicolo read the story. Twice Matteo wiped his eyes with his handkerchief. Watching him become emotional made me become emotional. When Nicolo had finished reading the article, he got up and kissed me on the forehead.

"You are a poet, Anna," Matteo said when he finished reading it, clearly moved by reading his own love story—the story of his life with Lenora.

"I am not a poet, Matteo, but your love story is pure poetry," I responded.

Then, we played cards.

— Chapter 14 —

A week later, on the morning of La Festa Degli Innamorati, I received two text messages as I awakened, one from Danielle and then one from Rosa.

Danielle's text read: *More hits on your Valentine's story than any other story so far this year. Lots of comments on the website. Be sure to take a look. Well done!!! Looking forward to more inspiring storytelling from Italy.*

Rosa's text read simple: *Call me when you are up.*

I dialed Rosa's number and she answered.

"Ah, pronto. Because you are alone, you will come and have dinner with us tonight. We will give you a big Valentine's hug," she said.

"Well, I'm kind of seeing someone—" I said.

"You've been here a month and you are already in a romance?"

"I think I may be," I told her. "With my neighbor Matteo's grandson."

"Your mother didn't say a word!" she said,

incredulously.

"I told her not to...not until I was sure."

"Your uncle will be glad to hear it," Rosa said, laughing.

"Tell him he's not a *perdente*," I said, laughing.

"I will tell him. And bring your Romeo to dinner, no?"

"Si," I said. "Can I bring a second date?"

"Oh, you are that popular that you have two Romeos?"

"Ha," I said. "No, but Matteo has become very dear to me."

"Of course! We have known him for years. We would love to see him."

As I was speaking with her, I heard shuffling outside my door, and I wondered if it was Matteo. Tossing on my robe, I walked to the foyer and saw a red envelope on the floor that had been slid under the door.

"Anna," it said on it.

I opened it.

It was a romantic card. Tucked inside the front cover in his handwriting was a short, handwritten poem.

My heart swelled, and I could definitely feel it beating. Nice. Strong. And hard.

My first love poem. How appropriate that I received it on February fourteenth—Lenora's favorite number—and on the day of love, from Nicolo.

The truth was, seven plus seven did equal fourteen, and suddenly, superstitions or no superstitions, everything in my world started to make sense to me.

—The End—

Special Thanks To ...

My special people and readers:
Amy Nelson
Doug Parrillo
Julie Wagner
Elizabeth Johnson
Leeanne Bell McManus
Leni Parrillo
Suzanne Rylee Ridolfi

Jo & Mark Verni for help with the Italian language.

And to my husband, Anthony,
for taking me to Siena, Italy,
to be with "my people" all those years ago.

Author's Note

I love Italy. My husband and I have been once for a two-week trip, and that was all it took for me to be under its spell.

What's not to love about Italy?

The people. The sights. The food. The wine.

Perhaps it helps that Italy is part of both of our families' heritage. There's an allure to it. And every time I watch a show about Italy on television where the host of the show is taking us through parts of countryside, I want to hop on a plane and go there.

In this story, it was fun to imagine myself as Anna. I've been lucky that I've had the opportunity to do some local travel writing here in Maryland. Those who get the opportunity to see the world are so lucky! It's a wonderful way to meet people and learn about cultures and traditions. Anna's opportunity to travel to Italy offered her the chance to not only learn about Italy's culture and people, but to get to know some folks even more intimately.

When my husband and I went to Italy, everywhere we went, we met people. Quite often while dining out, we would end up joining others and dining with them. People were so friendly and inviting. In Venice, we ended up having dinner with two women who wrote for PBS and two professors from Germany. It was one of our favorite nights, and I treasure those photographs and the memories I scribed in our travel journal.

If you get a chance to go to Italy, or if you are looking for your next place to visit, by all means, go.

As Anna discovered in her story, I do believe Italy is one of the most romantic places in the world.

xx,
Stephanie

A Little Bit About Writing Prompts

As a former full-time professor and now a part-time professor at a university in Maryland, I often use writing prompts in my classes. I also use them on my blog stephanieverni.com when I need to find my own inspiration.

Writing prompts can be so helpful. They can ignite an idea or help us flush out thoughts we may be having about a story we'd like to tackle.

Many times, these writing prompts—some as short as 300 words—can turn into something bigger...something longer...a novel or a novella or novelette.

Twice this has happened to me; *Little Milestones* grew out of a short story, and this little novelette that you read, *Anna in Tuscany*, grew out of a super short story I wrote and posted on my blog.

Sometimes, even when you write something short, you can't forget either the characters or the plot. The characters can haunt you until you sit down and give them room to grow.

When I wrote this short piece called *Franco and The Blonde*, it stayed with me. I couldn't quite shake the love Franco had for his wife, and how lonely he felt without her.

And while I did change the name of Franco to Matteo, and his son became his grandson, the premise was the same: a man whose wife died still loved and missed her. When the character of Anna popped into my head for a short story I had to write, I revisited *Franco and The Blonde*, and before long, *Anna in Tuscany* emerged.

All this to say the following: if you are a writer or an aspiring writer and you either (a) get stuck, (b) need inspiration, or (c) want to start a novel from scratch, sometimes prompts can help push you into a new realm.

There are many books devoted to writing prompts, but if you search online, you'll find loads of them...and perhaps one that suits you perfectly.

On the following pages you will see the original short story from which *Anna in Tuscany* was born.

Enjoy.

:-)

Franco and The Blonde

The old man sat at his window that overlooked the tiny, cobblestone street. The day had been long, and the sun had just set. He had eaten his pasta and gravy, the warmth of the summer day coming in through the window. Since he'd aged, he'd found himself not being as affected by the heat as he had been when Filomena was alive. She had despised the oppressive heat, and she would do her needlework right in front of the fan he'd bought for her.

The old man's window was open, and he sat in his worn, deep green chair, looking out the window and across the narrow road and into the window of the blonde woman's appartmento. He felt like an intruder, but it didn't stop him from watching her. Night after night, she would sit at the window of her dressing table, dry her long, blonde hair with a hairdryer, and then sit and curl it, her long locks cascading down her back and along the sides of her face.

His eyesight had grown weaker over the years, and yet, he could still follow her patterns nightly. It gave him great pleasure to watch her from his window; she never pulled down the blinds. Never. And so, each night, Franco would watch her from afar and reminisce.

Filomena's hair had been long and blonde as well. She hailed from Naples, and Franco and Filomena had met in Portofino on the beach over fifty years ago. He remembered watching her with her friends, wearing her blue checked bikini, passing a beach ball back and forth to each other, her blonde hair blowing in the summer breeze, her dark, big Sophia Loren glasses perched on her Roman nose. Some might not believe in love at first sight, but Franco knew immediately when he saw Filomena that something would pass between them. He would never admit to knowing they would marry and have a family, but deep down inside, he knew it to be true. Only Filomena knew the depth of his admiration and love for her that he felt immediately.

The glow of the light in the blonde's apartment flickered; Franco watched for her reaction. There was none. She turned to look behind her, and then, when the flash of darkness was over, she gazed back into the mirror that was in front of her and continued to curl her hair. Watching her each night had become a habit. He wondered about her, where she came from, who her family was, if she had a lover, and why she was here in Siena. She'd only lived in that appartmento for six months, and for six months Franco had been mesmerized.

She reminded him of Filomena in her twenties.

In fact, she reminded him of Filomena at every age—in her twenties, thirties, forties, fifties, and beyond.

Just then, there was a knock at the door. Franco was startled. He hadn't expected anyone. He had not been informed that someone was coming by. Perhaps one of his neighbors needed something.

Franco took one last look at the blonde, and hobbled out of his chair. He shuffled to the door and opened it.

"Hey, Papa," his son said. "I thought you might need a little company tonight."

"Ah, good, good," Franco said, patting his son on the back.

"And Mariana baked you some cookies. How about

a little card game?"

Franco looked at his son, and his son looked at Franco. His son caught a glimpse of the woman across the way and looked back at his father.

"You missing Mama tonight?" his son asked him.

"Always," Franco said, and his son wrapped him up in a hug that almost made Franco cry.

About the author

STEPHANIE VERNI is the author of THE LETTERS IN THE BOOKS (award winner for inspirational fiction, 2023); FROM HUMBUG TO HUMBLE: THE TRANSFORMATION OF EBENEZER SCROOGE; BENEATH THE MIMOSA TREE; INN SIGNIFICANT; LITTLE MILESTONES; THE POSTCARD; and ANNA IN TUSCANY. She is also a co-author of the textbook, EVENT PLANNING: COMMUNICATING THEORY & PRACTICE. Currently an adjunct professor at Stevenson University Online, she instructs communication courses for undergraduate and graduate students. She and her husband reside in Severna Park, Maryland, and have two children. On the side, she enjoys writing travel articles for Maryland Road Trips.

Visit her website at stephanieverni.com.

Book Awards:

THE LETTERS IN THE BOOKS, Bronze medal, Readers' Favorite, 2023.

THE POSTCARD AND OTHER SHORT STORIES & POETRY, Finalist, National Indie Excellence Awards, 2019.

INN SIGNIFICANT, Finalist, National Indie Excellence Awards 2017.

BASEBALL GIRL, Honorable Mention Award for Sports Fiction, Readers' Favorite, 2015.

BENEATH THE MIMOSA TREE, Bronze medal, Readers' Favorite, 2012; Finalist, National Indie Excellence Awards in 2013.,

Made in the USA
Middletown, DE
29 November 2025